Enid Blyton

The Crown of Gold

illustrated by
Rene Cloke

AWARD PUBLICATIONS LIMITED

Once upon a time there was a fairy who was very sad. He sat in a yellow celandine and swayed to and fro, thinking about everything. Two big tears rolled down his cheeks, and trickled down the stalk of the celandine.

'Oh dear, oh dear!' he sighed.

'Whatever is the matter?' said a brimstone butterfly, out for the first time that spring.

'Oh,' answered Casilda, the little fairy, 'I'm sad because I don't do anything as well as the other fairies can. I can't make beautiful dresses from morning mist like Sylfai, I can't paint the sunset pink, and I can't even hang the dewdrops on the grasses without spilling them.'

'That is very sad,' said the butterfly.
'But what does it matter?'

'Well, you see,' explained Casilda,
'every summer our King holds his court,
and gives little silver crowns set with
pearls to all those fairies who do beautiful
work. *All* my friends have got crowns, but
I never win one, however hard I try.'

'Cheer up,' said the butterfly, 'there
are other things worth while doing, even
if you don't win a crown for them!'

'Oh, *what*?' exclaimed Casilda.

THE CROWN OF GOLD

'Why, go into the world of boys and girls and see if you can't help the people there a bit,' said the butterfly. 'There are always lots of things to be done, even if you can't do them really well.'

'I'll go at once!' cried Casilda, standing up in the swaying celandine. 'Goodbye, yellow butterfly, and thank you!' Off he flew, out of Fairyland and into our world.

The first thing he came to was a clothes-line pegged with clothes. Mr Wind was tugging at one beautiful frock, and trying his hardest to pull it down into the mud.

'You *are* in a bad mood today, Mr Wind!' cried Casilda.

He flew on to the clothes-line and sat down by the frock, holding it tight. Mr Wind tugged and tugged, and very nearly made the little fairy tumble off. Then out of the house hobbled an old woman.

When she saw Casilda she cried out
with pleasure. 'Oh, thank you,' she said,
'if you hadn't held the frock on the line
for me, little fairy, the wind would have
whisked it away, and I should have had to
wash it clean again. My poor old back is
tired of stooping to wash, so thank you
very much.'

'Don't mention it,' called Casilda,
flying off again.

THE CROWN OF GOLD

The next day Casilda heard a tiny child crying bitterly because his balloon had blown away, and he could not reach it.

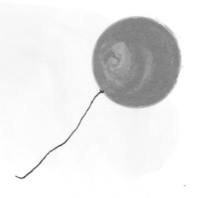

'Never mind,' said Casilda. 'Watch me get it!' and off he flew up into the air, caught the string, and flew down again.

The balloon came down with the string, and the child was delighted.

'Oh, thank you, dear little fairy,' he said gratefully.

'Don't mention it,' said Casilda, flying away.

Another time Casilda, peeping in at a window of a little house, saw a woman crying. She was holding her head, and saying, 'Oh, my head *does* hurt so.'

'Whatever can I do for her?' thought Casilda. 'I can't think of anything.' He looked round the room and noticed how dirty and dark it was.

'I know,' he thought, 'the room wants brightening up. I'll get some flowers.'

Off he flew to the meadows, and brought back a lovely bunch of golden buttercups and white daisies. He dropped them into the woman's lap. She was so astonished that she stopped crying, and forgot all about her bad headache.

'How lovely!' she cried. 'And how dark and dirty the room looks now with these bright flowers in it. I must hurry up and clean it.'

So she put the flowers in water, and started cleaning the room, singing cheerfully.

Casilda flew away feeling very pleased with himself. 'Tomorrow is the day our King holds his court and gives those lovely crowns,' he said to himself. 'I shall have to go, but I shan't mind a bit not winning a crown, because I've found something else I can do to make myself happy.'

Every fairy came to the King's palace the next day. The King was on his throne, and by him were many little silver crowns set with pearls. There was also one little golden crown set with diamonds, and Casilda wondered whether any of his friends had won it.

'Do you think you've won a crown this year?' asked Sylfai, the fairy dressmaker.

'Oh no,' answered Casilda, 'I know I haven't, because I've stopped doing beautiful things, and I live in the world of boys and girls now.'

Then the King made a speech, and said how glad he was to have the crowns to give to fairies who had done beautiful things that year.

THE CROWN OF GOLD

'Peronel,' he called. 'Here is a crown for you. You did a most beautiful thing when you painted the almond blossom such a lovely pink this spring.'

Peronel proudly received the crown.

'Morfael,' said the King. 'This crown is given to you for ringing the bluebells so sweetly at our last dance.'

Morfael went up for his crown most delighted. Then one by one the King gave out all the crowns except the gold one.

THE CROWN OF GOLD

'This crown,' he said, 'is for a little fairy who gave up doing beautiful things in Fairyland, but went all by himself into the world of boys and girls and did beautiful things there. He didn't think they were beautiful, but they were, and we are very proud of him. Casilda, here is your crown.'

THE CROWN OF GOLD

You can just imagine how pleased Casilda was, and what a lovely surprise he had. He is the only fairy in Fairyland who wears a golden crown, so if you meet a fairy wearing one, you will know at once that it is Casilda.

ISBN 0-86163-743-7

Text copyright Darrell Waters Limited
Illustrations copyright © 1995 Award Publications Limited

Enid Blyton's signature is a trademark of Darrell Waters Limited

First published in *Tarrydiddle Town Tales*

This edition first published 1995 by Award Publications Limited,
Goodyear House, 52–56 Osnaburgh Street, London NW1 3NS

Printed in Italy